Gigi & Jacques' Adventures in Paris

Written & Illustrated by
Maureen Edgecomb

PUBLISHED EXCLUSIVELY
for

Paris
LAS VEGAS

Published in the United States 2002
by Ravenwood Studios
P.O. Box 197
Diamond Springs, California 95619

Exclusively for
Park Place Entertainment Corporation

Gigi Paris and Jacques are trademarks of Park Place Entertainment Corporation

Book Design by Ruth Marcus, Sequim, WA

Printed in Hong Kong

First Edition

ISBN # 0-9718604-2-4

This book belongs to

Gigi loved her Paris.

Jacques loved his Paris, too.

Gigi's Paris was "très chic."

She had a nose for style.

Gigi was very, very fashionable.

Jacques' Paris was "bon magnifique."

He had a nose for creating masterpieces.

Jacques was very, very…well…Jacques.

Even though each knew a different Paris,
one day, they met in the park.

"Gigi, mon chéri, let me show you my Paris," Jacques said. "Oh, no Jacques, it isn't fashionable to go about without one's mistress," Gigi replied.

"C'mon, allons, let's go to Paris." "But how?" Gigi asked.

"I can get us into places. I can pull some strings." "We'll see about that," Gigi snapped.

And they slipped away…

...down the Champs Elysées

…through the Arc de Triomphe…

...to the cafés...

…and patisseries

...to fascinating places...

...bidding the shopkeepers "bonjour"...

…down the cobbled streets…

to see a mime fantastique…

to meet with their friends…

And together, they watched the sun set on their Paris.

But on their way home, the
streets looked different.

The shops were dark, with
no shopkeepers in sight.

Today became tonight, and all
was dark, cold, and lonely.

Nothing looked the same.

They were lost.

How could they find their way home
through the dark streets where they had never been?

Just then, Jacques spotted a large, empty basket.
"Entrez, Gigi, quickly, vite…we can stay warm in here."
Jacques knew that, with the sunrise, he could find their way home.

They soon fell asleep in the cold, Paris night.

It was almost tomorrow, when…

…they dreamed of clouds…and soft breezes…and fields to run in.

They dreamed of the Eiffel Tower and all their favorite places.

When suddenly the sun popped up,

Pardon!

and so did they!

"My dog!"   "Mon chien!"

"Jacques, Jacques, pull some strings!" Gigi barked.

So he did.

And they went down… down… down…

into the arms of Philippe and Claudette.

And Jacques & Gigi knew they would be spending
a lot more time together in their Paris.